Echoes of Reflection

Shelby Benson

"In the echoes of our struggles lies the strength to overcome, and in the reflection of our challenges, we find the resilience to rise."

Contents

Chapter 1
The Queen Bee

Sixteen-year-old Sydney Brown glided through the halls of Luxton High, her long brown hair cascading in silky waves down her back, the sunlight catching hints of caramel highlights as she moved. Each strand seemed perfectly placed, framing her heart-shaped face in a way that accentuated her natural beauty. Her hair was her crown, a symbol of her confidence and poise. Her big blue eyes sparkled with vitality and curiosity, drawing people in. They were like windows into her soul, revealing depths of emotion and intelligence that belied her youthful appearance. Sydney had a way of looking at people that made them feel seen and understood, a rare gift that endeared her to everyone she met. Despite her undeniable beauty, Sydney's appeal went beyond mere physical appearance. It was her aura of confidence and self-assuredness that truly set her apart. She carried herself with an air of grace and sophistication as if she were born to command attention and admiration.

Sydney wasn't the top student or the star athlete, but she didn't need accolades or trophies to validate her worth. Her charm and charisma were her greatest assets, effortlessly drawing people to her like moths to a flame. Whether she was engaging in lively conversation with her peers or lending a sympathetic ear to someone in need, Sydney had a way of making everyone feel welcome and accepted. As she eased her way through the halls of Luxton High, Sydney's presence was like a ray of sunshine on a cloudy day, brightening the spirits of those around her with her infectious smile and warm personality. She was the epitome of coolness and confidence, and though she may not be academically gifted or athletically inclined, Sydney's magnetic charm and ability to connect with people made her the undisputed queen bee of Luxton High. She didn't need hobbies or extracurricular activities to be popular, her mere presence was enough to captivate the hearts and minds of everyone she encountered.

"Hey, Sydney! Want to be partners in this stupid

group task?" Addison asked as they dawdled along to English, with no hesitation about the time it took to get there.

"Of course, anything to wind Mrs. Harrod up," Sydney replied with a smirking smile. Addison Moore was Sydney's closest friend. She had shiny blonde hair that flowed in golden waves around her shoulders, and it was as if her golden locks caught the sunlight, creating a halo of brilliance that framed her face like a radiant aura. Her striking green eyes sparkled with mischief and vitality, their vibrant hue drawing people in with their magnetic allure. Addison's appearance was as vivacious as her personality, each element coming together to create a picture of undeniable beauty and charm.

They had been inseparable since primary school, now navigating the social scene of Luxton High together. Their friendship was the foundation of their popularity. Addison's spirited personality and Sydney's natural leadership made them an unstoppable duo and… a major distraction in class.

As they entered the classroom, Sydney could feel the eyes of her classmates on her and Addi. They thrived for their attention, the subtle whispers, and the envious glances. It wasn't just their looks or their charm; it was their ability to make everyone feel seen, even if just for a moment. They were the sun, and everyone was caught in their orbit.

Mrs. Harrod, their English teacher, was used to Sydney and Addison's antics. She gave them a stern look as they took their seats, but there was a hint of amusement in her eyes. Sydney knew that despite their occasional mischief, the teachers knew they were both good students who could deliver when it mattered.

During the lesson, Sydney found it hard to focus. Her mind wandered to the upcoming weekend and the party that she and Addison had been invited to. It was supposed to be the event of the month, and Sydney was already planning what to wear and how to make a grand entrance.

She glanced at Addison, who was doodling hearts into her notebook and gave her a nudge. "Hey, what are you wearing to Jenna's party?" Sydney whispered.

Addison grinned. "I'm thinking that new dress I bought last week. You?" Sydney leaned back, contemplating. "Don't know." "You should wear that red one!" "Girls, no talking in class, please," Mrs. Harrod snapped, bringing both their attention back to the lesson. But as the lesson dragged on, Sydney's thoughts kept drifting, lunch couldn't come quick enough. When the bell finally rang, she and Addison were the first out of the classroom, making their way to their usual spot in the dining hall.

Lunch was spent with their friends, chatting about the latest gossip and upcoming events. Sydney loved the attention, the admiration. She was the queen bee after all, and Addison was her trusted confidant. Together, they set trends and defined what was cool at Luxton High. Their table buzzed with excitement as they discussed the party and who was dating whom.

"Did you hear about Emily and Jack?" one of their friends, Olivia, whispered conspiratorially. "Apparently, they were caught making out behind the sports hall."

"No way!" Addison exclaimed, her eyes widening. "I thought Jack was with Hannah."

"He was," Olivia confirmed. "But I guess things changed."

Sydney leaned back, smirking. "I knew something was up. Jack's been acting weird around Hannah for weeks."

The gossip flowed freely; each story more sensational than the last. Sydney thrived in this environment, where her opinions and insights were valued. As she was the queen bee, her court hung on her every word.

After school, they would usually hang out at

Addison's house, binge-watching their favourite shows, or discussing the latest school drama. They had a bond that went beyond superficial. They shared secrets, supported each other through family troubles, and celebrated each other's successes.

But even though Sydney lived a perfect life, she would still get this nagging feeling every night before bed. The feeling would creep up on her only when she was alone, when there were no distractions of gossip or admiration, and most importantly, when her popularity did not matter.

The feeling ached in her chest and crawled its way up to her head, gnawing at her mind while she tried so hard to shut off her thoughts and go to sleep. There was only one word to describe this feeling. A word that has been haunting her for quite some time now.

Emptiness.

When she felt this way, she sometimes wondered if there was more to life than just being popular. Addison had always been there to lift her spirits, but lately, even that seemed different. There was a distance growing between them, an unspoken tension that Sydney couldn't quite understand. As she stared at the ceiling, her phone buzzed with a message from Addison.

Addison: "Can't wait for the party! It's going to be epic!"

Sydney: "Totally! We're going to own that place!"

She put her phone down and sighed. The excitement for the party was real, but so was the sense of unease. Was this all there was to life? Parties, popularity, and the endless quest to stay on top? Sydney had everything she thought she wanted, but why did she feel like something was missing?

Her thoughts were interrupted by a knock on her door.

Her mother peeked in, a warm smile on her face. Sydney's mom, Rachel, was a petite woman with blonde hair styled into a neat, fringed bob. She wore a crisp white shirt tucked into a pencil skirt, her professional attire at odds with the fatigue evident on her face. Despite her small stature, Rachel exuded an aura of immense strength and kindness. Her hands, though small, were always gentle, whether she was typing at her desk or comforting her daughter.

"How was school today, honey?" she asked, stepping inside. "Same as always," Sydney replied, forcing a smile. "Just getting ready for Jenna's party this weekend."

Her mother sat at the end of her bed, understanding the look in her daughter's eyes. She always knew when something was up, and it seemed she always knew just what to say, as if she could read minds. "You know, Sydney, it's okay to want more than just popularity. There's so much out there to explore and experience."

Sydney nodded, though she wasn't sure how to explain the emptiness she felt. "I know, Mom. It's just... I don't know. I feel like something is missing."

Her mom gave her a reassuring hug. "You'll figure it out. You're smart, capable and have the whole world waiting for you beyond high school."

As her mother left, Sydney pondered her words. Maybe it was time to find something more meaningful, something that went beyond the surface. But for now, she had a party to think about and a reputation to maintain. As she drifted off to sleep, Sydney could still feel the growing unease she couldn't quite place. The life she had built seemed perfect on the outside. But on the inside, she yearned for something deeper, something real. Little did she know, the events about to unfold would challenge her in ways she never imagined.

Chapter 2
The Argument

The next day at school, during lunch, Sydney and Addison found themselves at odds. They were standing by the lockers, with the usual buzz of Luxton High filling the background.

"Let's go to the AstroTurf and watch the boys play football," Addison suggested, her green eyes sparkling with excitement.

Sydney shook her head, frowning slightly. "I'd rather stay in the hall. It's too cold outside, and besides, I have no interest in watching them."

Addison's smile faded. "Come on, Syd, it'll be fun. We never do this together anymore."

Sydney crossed her arms. "I just don't feel like it, okay?"

Addison's patience snapped. "The only reason you won't go is because your boyfriend is being weird! You've been avoiding everyone just to deal with him."

Sydney's eyes widened, hurt and anger flashing over her face, partly because she agreed. She had been dating Landon Smit for two years but recently had felt the connection between them fading, but didn't want to admit this amongst the group. "That's not true! You have no idea what you're talking about."

Addison shot back, frustration evident in her voice. "Maybe I do! You've changed, Syd. It's like you don't care about anything anymore unless it's about him,"

Without another word, Sydney turned on her heel and stormed off, her heart pounding with a mixture of betrayal and agony. She marched down the hallway, her vision blurring slightly as she tried to hold back the tears.

As Sydney stormed away from Addison, the echoes of their argument lingered in the hallway. Her heart pounded in her chest, the hurt of Addison's accusations stinging like a fresh wound. Yet, amidst the anger, there was a flicker of guilt. Maybe Addison was right. Maybe she had been neglecting their friendship, too preoccupied with her own problems. Sydney found herself in an empty corridor, her steps slowing as the weight of Addison's words settled upon her. She leaned against the cold metal of the lockers, her mind racing with thoughts of Landon and their strained relationship. It had been weeks since they had shared a genuine conversation, their once strong bond crumbling under the weight of unspoken tension. But was that really a reason to abandon Addison? Sydney shook her head, pushing away the guilt that threatened to consume her. She had her own problems to deal with, her own life to live. Addison couldn't expect her to drop everything just to cater to her needs. Yet, even as she rationalised her actions, Sydney couldn't shake the feeling of emptiness that tore at her from within. She missed the easy laughter, the shared secrets, the unspoken understanding that had always defined her friendship with Addison. But now, it seemed like all of that was slipping away, lost amongst their argument. Sydney closed her eyes, wishing the tears that threatened to fall to stay at bay. She couldn't afford to show weakness, not now, not when everything felt like it was falling apart. Taking a deep breath, she pushed herself off the lockers and continued down the hallway, her steps heavy with the weight of unresolved emotions.

Her head throbbed with a dull ache, the remnants of her argument with Addison still fresh in her mind. She couldn't shake the feeling that she made a mistake, that she had pushed away the one person who had always been there for her. But as numbness spread across her face and her vision began to blur, Sydney realised that her problems with Addison were the last of her worries. Something was seriously wrong, and she needed help. With a sinking feeling in her chest, she stumbled into the medical room, catching the attention of the school nurse, Mrs. Thomson.

"Sydney, are you okay?" Mrs. Thomson asked, rushing to her side.

"I don't... I don't feel well," Sydney managed to say, but her words came out slurred, her tongue feeling heavy and uncooperative.

Mrs. Thomson guided her to a chair, her concern growing. "Stay with me, Sydney. Can you tell me what's wrong?"

"My head... it hurts... I can't see properly," Sydney mumbled, her panic rising. The numbness in her face was spreading, and her limbs felt weak and uncoordinated.

Mrs. Thomson's expression turned serious as she

called for an ambulance. "It's going to be okay Sydney; help is on the way."

As Sydney sat there, her vision fading in and out, she could only think of one person: Addison. Despite their argument, all she wanted was her best friend by her side. The fear of what was happening to her over-shadowed the anger and hurt she had felt just moments before.

"Addi... I need Addison," she whispered, hoping Mrs. Thomson could understand her garbled words.

"Don't worry, Sydney. We'll get her," Mrs. Thomson assured, sending a student to find Addison.

As her head spun with pain and confusion, a feeling of vulnerability washed over her. She felt small and fragile, like a ship lost at sea in the midst of a raging storm. Minutes felt like hours as Sydney waited for Addison to arrive, her heart pounding with anticipation. The fear of facing whatever was happening to her alone clawed at her insides, but she clung to the hope that her best friend would come to her rescue. Then, like a ray of sunshine breaking through the clouds, Addison burst into the medical room, her face pale with worry. Sydney's heart skipped a beat at the sight of her, relief flooding as Addison rushed to her side.

"Syd! Oh my God, what happened?" Sydney

reached out weakly, relief flooding her as Addison took her hand. "I'm here, Syd. I'm here," Addison said with tears in her eyes.

The ambulance arrived, and as Sydney lay on the stretcher, her mind racing, paramedics sprang into action with practice efficiency. Their movements were swift and purposeful, their voices calm and reassuring as they worked to assess Sydney's condition and provide the necessary care. One paramedic leaned over to Sydney, gently probing her forehead and temples, checking for signs of injury or trauma. Another took her blood pressure, his fingers softly wrapping the cuff around her arm as he listened intently to the rhythmic thumping of her pulse. A third paramedic hovered nearby, a medley of medical equipment at their disposal, ready to assist their colleagues in whatever way necessary. As they worked, the paramedics asked Sydney a series of questions, their voices gentle and reassuring as they tried to piece together the puzzle of her symptoms. They asked about her medical history, pre-existing conditions she might have, and any medications she might be taking. Sydney did her best to answer, her words slurred and disjointed as she struggled to make sense of the chaos in her mind.

Throughout it all, Addison remained by Sydney's

side, her presence a constant source of control during the craziness. "I'm right here with you Syd," Addison said, her voice steady despite tears streaming down her face. She held Sydney's hand tightly, her fingers interwind with Sydney's as they both clung to each other for support.

As the paramedics continued their assessment, they carefully monitored Sydney's vital signs, checking her heart rate, respiratory rate, and oxygen saturation levels. They adjusted the flow of oxygen through the mask that covered Sydney's nose and mouth, ensuring that she was getting enough air to breathe as they worked to stabilize her condition. Once they had gathered the necessary information, the paramedics decided to transport Sydney to the hospital for further evaluation and treatment. With meticulous accuracy, they lifted Sydney onto a gurney and secured her in place, ensuring she was stable and comfortable for the journey ahead.

As they wheeled Sydney out to the waiting ambulance, the paramedics maintained a constant dialogue with each other, their voices calm and steady as they relayed vital information to the hospital staff awaiting their arrival. Sydney's heart raced with fear and uncertainty, but she drew strength on the fact she was in good hands, surrounded by a team of skilled professionals dedicated to her care. As the ambulance pulled away from school, sirens blaring and lights flashing, Sydney closed her eyes and focused on the steady heartbeat, praying for strength and courage for what lay ahead. Sydney's thoughts drifted back to the argument. She realised how trivial it seemed now, how much she needed Addison. The fear of the unknown loomed large, but with Addison by her side, holding her hand tightly and offering words of reassurance, Sydney felt a glimmer of hope.

Chapter 3
The Hospital

The ambulance came to a halt outside the emergency entrance, its flashing lights casting an eerie glow on the surroundings. Sydney's heart raced as she was wheeled out on a stretcher, her body feeling fragile, and her mind overwhelmed by a whirlwind of emotions. Despite the chaos, she caught sight of her mom and stepdad standing just outside, their faces etched with worry.

"Mom! Andy!" Sydney's voice was barely a whisper, but it carried a sense of urgency that spurred her mom into action. Sydney's mom rushed forward, her arms outreached in a gesture of comfort and relief. Her hazelnut eyes usually filled with a spark of joy, now brimmed with tears, reflecting the depth of concern for Sydney.

Her stepdad, Andy, followed close behind, his expression a mix of concern and determination.

Andy was a steady, reliable figure. Medium height and broad-shouldered, he exuded a quiet strength that had been a source of comfort for Sydney since she was five years old. His soft brown hair was slightly dishevelled from running his hands through it in worry, and his blue eyes mirrored the same concern that Rachel's did. Andy was an electrician by trade, methodical and logical, but in moments like this, his calm demeanour and reassuring presence were what Sydney needed most.

"We're here, sweetheart," Rachel murmured, her voice trembling with emotion as she enveloped Sydney in a tight embrace. Andy placed a reassuring hand on Sydney's shoulder, his touch a comforting reminder that she was not alone in this ordeal. As the paramedics wheeled Sydney into the hospital, her mom and stepdad followed closely behind, their presence a source of comfort in unfamiliar surroundings. Together, they navigated the maze of corridors and bustling hallways until they reached the emergency triage area. Addison remained by her side, offering silent support and a reassuring smile. Despite the tension in the air, there was a sense of solidarity between them, an understanding that they would weather this storm together.

The emergency room was a hive of activity, with doctors and nurses rushing to and from, their faces masked in concentration as they tended to the steady stream of patients. Sydney's mom and stepdad hovered anxiously nearby, their eyes never leaving her as she underwent a series of tests and examinations. Hours passed in a blur as Sydney was poked and prodded, her body feeling increasingly weary with each passing moment.

"You're doing great, sweetheart," Rachel assured, squeezing Sydney's hand.

"We're right here with you." Andy nodded, his calm voice a steady anchor in a storm of confusion. "Just focus on getting better, Syd. We'll handle everything else."

As the night wore on, Sydney's exhaustion began to catch up with her, her eyelids growing heavy with fatigue. She could feel the weight of the day's events bearing down on her, the uncertainty of her condition looming large in her mind. But amidst the chaos and confusion, there was a glimmer of hope: the unwavering love and support of her family and friends. They were her rock, her anchor in a sea of uncertainty, and she knew that as long as they were by her side, she could face whatever lay ahead. As the hours stretched into the early morning, Rachel and Andy took turns sitting vigil by her bedside, their presence a comfort in the dimly lit hospital room. Addison remained close by, giving Sydney a reassuring smile whenever she stirred restlessly in her sleep. Despite the exhaustion that threatened to overwhelm her, Sydney found solace in the knowledge that she was not alone. As she drifted off into a fitful sleep, her mind filled with fragmented dreams and half-thoughts, she clung to her family's presence. Rachel's voice, soft and soothing, broke through the haze of Sydney's thoughts.

"I remember when you were little, you used to be so brave. You'd climb everything, and ride your bike without training wheels, and never once did you cry when you fell. You've always had an incredible strength, Sydney. And you're showing it now."

The morning brought a flurry of activity as doctors and nurses checked on Sydney's condition. Dr. Johnson, a middle-aged man with kind eyes and a reassuring demeanour, took charge of her case. He explained that they were running a series of tests to determine the cause of her symptoms and that it was crucial for her to rest and remain calm.

"We're going to take care of you, Sydney," Dr.

Johnson said, his voice steady and comforting. "You have a strong support system here, and that will make all the difference."

Throughout the day, Sydney underwent a further battery of tests: blood work, CT scans, and neurological assessments. The medical staff moved with cracticid efficiency, their actions swift and precise. Sydney felt a mix of fear and gratitude as she was wheeled from one procedure to the next, her family and Addison always close by.

The CT scan was particularly daunting, the loud clanging of the machine echoing in her ears as she lay still, her mind racing with thoughts of what might be wrong. But she focussed on the comforting companionship of her family.

As the hours passed, the waiting became almost unbearable. Sydney's mind was a whirlwind of emotions, the uncertainty weighing heavily on her.

In the late afternoon, Dr. Johnson returned with the results of the tests. His expression was serious but not without a glimmer of hope. "Sydney, we've found the cause of your symptoms," he began, his voice calm and measured. "You have had a stroke, but we don't yet know the exact cause. Because of your age, we are optimistic about your recovery. We've started you on blood-thinning medication to prevent any further incidents and to help your body heal."

The room fell silent as Dr. Johnson explained the situation in more detail. He reassured them that while it was a serious condition, it was treatable with the right medical care. Sydney listened intently, her mind absorbing the information. She felt a mixture of relief and fear, but most of all, she felt a sense of determination. She was ready to overcome this.

The things that seemed important a few days ago were the last things on her mind. The party that Jenna had invited her to, her relationship with her boyfriend, her popularity in school, the nagging feeling of emptiness that would creep up on her late at night. None of it seemed real anymore. It was like that version of herself was gone, replaced by this new version of herself that now lay weak in a hospital bed.

Within the next few days, Sydney was started on blood-thinning medication to reduce the possibility of another stroke occurring. She underwent regular checks to monitor her progress. And as the days passed, Sydney began to show signs of improvement. The medication started to take effect and her symptoms gradually lessened, and she began to feel more like herself.

Dr. Johnson was pleased with Sydney's progress

and agreed to discharge her to continue her recovery at home.

Sydney's heart was filled with gratitude, utterly excited as she and her family prepared to leave the hospital.

As they pulled into the driveway of their home, Sydney noticed the lights on in the living room. At first, she wondered who was inside, but then she saw a familiar van parked on the curb, and she was suddenly overcome with excitement. Waiting anxiously for her arrival were her two older brothers, Noah and Brandon. They both lived about half an hour away, and with their jobs and her school, Sydney and her brothers rarely saw each other anymore. Noah, ten years older than Sydney, was a big teddy bear of a man. Standing at six feet with a chubby build, he had always been her protector growing up. His dark brown hair and kind brown eyes gave him a warm, approachable appearance, despite his imposing stature. Brandon, eight years older than Sydney, was smaller in stature but no less fierce in his love for her. He was about four inches shorter than Noah, and half his weight. He had more of an athletic build, with short, dirty brown hair and hazel eyes that always sparkled with either mischief or kindness. Despite their difference in appearance, both brothers shared a deep bond with Sydney, having been her constant companions and protectors since she was a little girl, starting ten years ago when their parents got divorced.

As Sydney stepped through the front door, her brothers cheered and rushed to her side. Noah enwrapped her in a gentle bear hug, being careful not to squeeze her too tightly.

"Hey, trouble," he said softly, his voice filled with emotion. "How are you holding up?"

"I'm okay," Sydney replied, her voice muffled against his chest. "I'm better now that I'm back home with both of you."

Brandon put his arms around her, his eyes searching her face for any sign of distress. "We're so proud of you, Syd," he said. "We know how hard it must be to deal with something like this."

Sydney smiled, feeling the warmth of her family's love surrounding her. "Thank you, both of you. I couldn't get through this without all of you supporting me."

The three siblings stood there for a moment, basking in the comfort of each other's presence. Despite the challenges that lay ahead, Sydney knew she could face them with the constant backing of her family.

Chapter 4
A Bittersweet Revelation

As Sydney continued her journey of recovery from the comfort of her own bed, she faced a new challenge that shook her to the core. One afternoon, as she sat in her bedroom, Addison entered with a heavy heart, her expression reflecting the weight of the news she bore.

"Hey, Syd," Addison said softly, her voice tinged with sadness as she took a seat beside her.

Sydney looked up, sensing the gravity of the moment. "What's wrong?"

Addison took a deep breath, her eyes filled with regret. "I have to transfer to a different school," she confessed, her voice barely above a mutter.

Sydney's heart sank at the revelation. "You're leaving?" she asked, disbelief colouring her words.

Addison nodded; her gaze fixed on the floor. "Yeah. I can't keep up with the grades here, and my parents think it's best if I go somewhere else." Sydney's mind reeled with the implications of Addison's departure. She couldn't imagine facing her recovery without her best friend by her side, but she knew that Addison's education was important.

"I understand," Sydney said, her voice choked with emotion. "But I'll miss you."

Addison reached out, taking Sydney's hand in hers. "I'll always be your best friend, Syd," she promised, "Even though I won't be at the same school anymore, I'll always be here for you." Tears welled up in Sydney's eyes as she squeezed Addison's hand tightly, the ache of their impending separation settling in her chest. They sat in silence for a moment, the weight of Addison's departure hanging heavy in the air. "I wish things could be different," Sydney murmured, her voice thick with emotion. Addison nodded, her eyes brimming with tears. "Me too, Syd. But no matter where we go, you'll always be my sister." With a heavy heart, Sydney braced herself for the inevitable goodbye, knowing that even though Addison might be changing schools, their friendship would always remain a cherished and irreplaceable part of her life. As they faced the uncertain future together, Sydney took comfort in the knowledge that no matter where life took them, their bond would never be broken.

The days following Addison's revelation were filled with a mix of melancholy and determination for Sydney. She was still reeling from the news but focused on her recovery. Her mom and stepdad provided unwavering support, helping her with her physical therapy exercises and ensuring she took her medication on time.

One evening, while Rachel was preparing dinner, Sydney found herself lost in thought, staring out the window at the setting sun. The vibrant hues of orange and pink painted the sky, reminding her of the many sunsets she had shared with Addison. Her heart ached at the thought of facing those moments alone.

Rachel noticed her daughter's distant expression and approached her gently. "Hey, sweetheart, are you okay?"

Sydney sighed, turning to face her mom. "It's just... It's hard to accept the fact that Addison is leaving Luxton High. I know she has to, but it's not fair."

Rachel sat down beside her, wrapping an arm around her shoulders. "I know it's tough, honey. Change is never easy, especially when it involves someone you care about so deeply. But you're strong, and your friendship with Addison is strong, too. You'll find ways to stay connected."

Sydney nodded, drawing comfort from her mom's words. "I guess. I just can't imagine not seeing her every day."

Rachel squeezed her shoulder. "You two have been through so much together. This is just another challenge you'll overcome. And remember, we are all here for you."

As the days passed, Sydney and Addison made the most of the time they had left spending everyday together. They spent afternoons reminiscing about their favourite memories, scrolling through their Snapchat photos filled with snippets of their adventures. They laughed and cried, cherishing every moment as they faced the impending separation.

One particular wintery afternoon, Sydney felt strong enough to leave her house for the first time in a while and visit the park down the road with Addison. It took a lot of mental and physical strength to get dressed for the cold and walk there, but Addison helped her. The walk took longer than it normally did, before the incident, but it was worth visiting their favourite place. A place filled with memories of care-free days, swinging on swings, and getting up to no good. As they walked through the park, they talked about their hopes and dreams for the future.

"Syd, promise me one thing," Addison said, her voice serious.

"Anything," she replied.

"Promise me you won't give up on your dreams, no matter what happens. You've always been so passionate and driven. Don't let anything take that away from you."

Sydney smiled, feeling a renewed sense of determination. "I promise, Addi. And you promise me the same."

Addison grinned. "Deal."

As the day of Addison's transfer approached, Sydney found herself grappling with a mix of emotions. She was proud of Addison for prioritizing her education but couldn't shake the sadness of saying goodbye.

The night before Addison was set to start her new school, the two friends decided to have a sleepover, just like they used to when they were kids. They stayed up late watching their favourite movies and sharing their deepest fears and hopes for the future. It was a night filled with laughter and tears, a testament to the depth of their bond.

The next morning, Addison left for her new

school, but she and Sydney made a pact to meet whenever they could at Addison's house. This gave them something to look forward to and a way to maintain their close connection.

The days following Addison's transfer were challenging for Sydney. She felt a deep sense of loss but channelled her energy into her recovery. Rachel and Andy continued to be a pillar of support, helping her stay on track with her physical therapy and medication.

One afternoon, as Sydney was working on her exercises, her phone buzzed with a message from Addison. It was a picture of her new school, accompanied by a text that read, "Thinking of you. Miss you already." Sydney smiled, feeling a warmth spread over her chest. She quickly replied, "Miss you too. Hope you have the best day!"

As Sydney sat alone in her room, her thoughts drifted back to a time when she and Addison had ruled Luxton High with ease. They had been inseparable, their bond unbreakable as they navigated the intricate social dynamics of high school together. Popularity had come effortlessly to them, their natural charisma and magnetic personalities drawing others into their orbit. But now, as Sydney reflected on the events of the past few weeks, she couldn't help but feel a sense of disillusionment. Despite their once-close friendships, none of her other friends had stepped up to support her during her time of need. They had all drifted away, leaving Sydney feeling abandoned and alone. Even her boyfriend, Landon, had turned his back on her when she needed him the most. His absence had left a gaping void in Sydney's life, one that she wasn't sure how to fill. And then there were the messages. Every day, Sydney was bombarded with texts and calls from people who claimed to be her friends. But she couldn't shake the feeling that their concern was superficial, that they were only reaching out to satisfy their curiosity or to get the latest gossip about her condition.

It was a harsh realisation, one that left Sydney feeling more isolated than ever before. She had always prided herself on her popularity, on her ability to command attention and respect wherever she went. But now, as she sat alone, she couldn't help but wonder if it had all been an illusion. With a heavy heart, Sydney pushed her thoughts aside and focused on the one person who had never let her down: Addison. Despite the physical distance between them, Sydney knew that Addison was always just a phone call away, ready to offer support and comfort whenever she needed it. As Sydney reached for her phone, a sense of gratitude washed over her. In a world full of superficial friendships and broken promises, Addison's constant loyalty was a beacon of hope in the darkness. As Sydney dialled her friend's number, she knew that no matter what challenges lay ahead, she would face them with Addison by her side.

Chapter 5
New Year New Me?

Ew Year's Eve arrived with a mix of excitement and trepidation for Sydney. It marked her first big social event since her stroke, and she couldn't help but feel a sense of anticipation tinged with anxiety. Despite Addison's persuasion to attend the party with their old friends and Landon, Sydney couldn't shake off the apprehension that gnawed at her insides. The evening started with Sydney meticulously selecting her outfit. She rifled through her wardrobe, finally settling on the stunning red dress she had originally planned to wear to Jenna's party. The one she had missed due to her illness. Tonight, she decided, she would reclaim that missed opportunity, wearing the dress as a symbol of resilience and defiance against the setbacks she had faced. As Sydney slipped into the red dress, she couldn't help but feel a surge of determination coursing through her veins. This party would mark a new beginning, a chance for her to leave the hardships of the past behind and embrace the promise of the future.

Arriving at the party venue, Sydney was greeted by familiar sights and sounds of celebration. The room was abuzz with laughter and chatter as friends and acquaintances mingled, their faces lit up with excitement for the night ahead. As Sydney made her way through the crowd, she felt a mixture of excitement and nerves bubbling within her. She exchanged hugs and greetings with familiar faces, catching up on the latest gossip and sharing laughs with old friends.

But amidst the joyous atmosphere, Sydney couldn't shake off the nagging feeling that something was amiss. It was as if a dark cloud hung over the festivities, casting a shadow of doubt over her newfound sense of optimism. It was Addison who noticed it first. As Sydney chatted with a group of friends, Addison's sharp eyes caught sight of something that made her pause... a bald patch on Sydney's head, stark against the backdrop of her flowing locks. Addison's expression turned to one of concern as she reached out to touch Sydney's hair, her touch gentle yet firm.

"Syd, wait," she said softly, her voice filled with apprehension.

Sydney froze, her heart pounding in her chest as Addison's fingers brushed up against her scalp. There was a moment of stunned silence as Sydney processed what Addison had discovered.

A cold knot formed in the pit of her stomach as she reached up to feel the spot Addison was referring to. Sure enough, her fingers encountered a smooth, bare patch of skin where her hair should have been.

Panic surged through Sydney as she grappled with the implications of Addison's discovery. Could this be related to her recent health issues? Was it a sign of something more serious lurking beneath the surface? With a sinking heart, Sydney realised that she couldn't ignore the truth any longer. Her recovery from the stroke had been a long and arduous journey, but this new symptom threatened to unravel all the progress she had made. Despite the overwhelming sense of fear and uncertainty that washed over her, Sydney flipped her hair to the side in hopes her locks would cover the bald spot and forced a smile as she mingled with her friends at the New Year's Eve party. She couldn't bring herself to confide in anyone else about what Addison had found, not feeling close enough to any of them, since none had truly been there for her so far in her recovery.

As the night wore on, and the clock ticked closer to midnight, Sydney's mind was consumed by thoughts of the bald patch and what it could mean for her future. She tried to push aside her fears and enjoy the festivities, but the nagging worry refused to be silenced. It wasn't until Addison confronted her about the bald patch that Sydney's façade began to crack. The concern in Addison's eyes mirrored Sydney's inner turmoil, and for a moment, Sydney allowed herself to acknowledge the gravity of the situation. With tears welling up in her eyes, Sydney confided in Addison about her fears and insecurities. She spoke of her struggle with the aftermath of the stroke, the uncertainty of what lay ahead, and the overwhelming sense of isolation amidst the crowd of partygoers. To her relief, Addison listened with empathy and understanding, offering words of comfort and support. She assured Sydney that she wasn't alone in her struggles and that she had a friend who deeply cared about her well-being. As the countdown to midnight began and the cheers erupted around them, Sydney found solace in the warmth of Addison's embrace, but she couldn't shake the feeling of foreboding that lingered over her.

The New Year was supposed to herald a fresh start, but for Sydney, it felt like the beginning of a new nightmare, one filled with uncertainty and challenges she wasn't ready to face alone. With a heavy heart, Sydney braced herself for the days ahead, knowing that the road to recovery would be fraught with obstacles, both seen and unseen.

As the party wound down and guests began to depart, Sydney found herself lost in thought. She watched as her friends said their goodbyes and made plans for the rest of the night, but her mind was elsewhere, consumed by the unsettling discovery of the bald patch on her head. As she bid farewell to the last guests and made her way home with Addison by her side, Sydney felt nothing but dread. The events of the evening had left her feeling shaken and vulnerable, and she knew that she couldn't simply ignore the issue at hand.

Once they were alone, Addison turned to Sydney with a worried expression. "Syd, are you okay?" she asked softly, her voice filled with concern.

Sydney forced a smile, but it faltered as she met Addison's gaze. "I don't know, Addi," she admitted, her voice trembling slightly. "I'm scared."

Addison reached out, wrapping an arm around Sydney's shoulders in a gesture of comfort. "It's going to be okay, Syd," she said reassuringly. "We'll figure this out together."

Sydney nodded, grateful for Addison's support, but her mind was still reeling with unanswered questions. The uncertainty buried at her insides, filling her with a sense of dread.

As she arrived home, Sydney retreated to her room, seeking solace in the familiar surroundings. She sank onto her bed, her thoughts consumed by the events of the evening. She reached up to touch the bald patch on her head, her fingers tracing the smooth, bare skin with a mixture of fascination and fear. The room was filled with a heavy silence as Sydney wrestled with her emotions. She felt a wave of frustration wash over her, frustration with her vulnerability, frustration at the uncertainty of her health, and frustration at the unfairness of it all. But amidst the frustration, there was a glimmer of determination to face whatever life throws her way with courage and resilience. Sydney knew that she couldn't let her fear hold her back, that she had to confront the issue head-on and seek answers.

Chapter 6
A Difficult Conversation

ew Year's Day dawned bright and hopeful, but for Sydney, it quickly took a turn for the worse. She was finally reuniting with her dad and stepfamily after a long while, a reunion that she had both anticipated and dreaded. Once upon a time, she had been a daddy's girl, basking in his attention and affection. However, as the years had gone by, his attention had gradually shifted towards his new wife and stepchildren. The distance that had grown between them left Sydney feeling like a stranger in her father's house. Sydney's heart pounded as she walked into her dad's, memories of the better days flooding her mind. Her stepmom, a cheerful woman named Brenda, greeted her with a hug. Her stepsisters, Tilly and Carla, paused their phones to welcome her with bright smiles and waves. Her dad, Larry, an average-height man with a warm demeanour, was busy preparing drinks in the kitchen, his back turned to her.

"Hey, Dad," Sydney said, trying to keep her voice steady.

Her dad turned around; his smile broad and genuine. "Hey, Syd! Good to see you, kiddo!" he said, pulling her into a loving but almost obligatory hug.

As the family gathered in the living room, Sydney felt an increasing sense of dread. The previous night's discovery of a bald patch on her head was weighing heavily on her mind, and she knew she needed to confide in her dad about her new symptoms. But the fear of his reaction consumed her.

"Dad, can I talk to you for a minute?" she asked, her voice trembling slightly.

"Sure, Syd. What's on your mind?" he replied, still smiling as he turned his attention to her.

Sydney glanced around nervously, noticing the curious but concerned glances from Brenda, Tilly and Carla. She wished for a private moment, but she knew she had to get it out now. "Something happened last night," she began, her voice barely above a whisper. "I was at a party and one of my friends noticed a bald patch on my head."

Her dad's expression shifted slightly, a flicker of concern crossing his face, but it was quickly replaced by a grin. "Well, everyone, make sure you don't stress Sydney out too much, or we'll have a load of sweeping up to do!" he joked lightly, his voice echoing in the room.

Sydney felt the blood drain from her face. The room erupted in soft, awkward chuckles, but all she could hear was the pounding of her heart. Her eyes filled with tears, and she couldn't bring herself to look at her dad. "Dad, this isn't a joke. I'm really scared," she said, her voice breaking.

Her dad's smile faded slightly, replaced by a slight look of concern. "Oh, Syd, I didn't realise it was that serious. You will be perfectly fine," he said patting her shoulder gently. "And if it doesn't grow back, you'll just look more like me," he added, trying to lighten the mood.

Sydney's frustration boiled over. "You don't understand, Dad. This isn't just about hair. It's about my health, my future. I need you to take this seriously," she pleaded, her tears spilling over.

Her dad sighed, running his hand over his face. "I get that you're worried, but you're young and healthy. You'll bounce back from this," he said dismissively.

Sydney clenched her fists, feeling a wave of anger

and despair. "I need your support, not your jokes," she said, her voice shaking.

Her dad looked at her, his eyes softening slightly. "Okay, I'm sorry if I made light of it. I'm here for you, Syd." His words were slightly more reassuring but still lacking the true warmth and reassurance she so desperately needed.

Feeling somewhat overwhelmed, Sydney excused herself from the gathering. As she walked away, she could hear Brenda gently reminding her dad to be more sensitive. Her mind was spinning with a whirlwind of emotions. She knew that her dad loved her, and that humour was his way of dealing with difficult news, but she could not help but wish for a more straightforward show of support in her time of need. As she rushed home, her thoughts raced ahead to the conversation she knew she had to have with her mom and stepdad. How could she tell them about her new symptoms? How could she find the words to convey the gravity of her situation, the fear and uncertainty that consumed her? With trembling hands and a heavy heart, Sydney entered the familiar warmth of her home, the comforting embrace of her family's love offering a fleeting respite from the storm raging inside her. But as she gathered her courage to speak, she felt the weight of her words pressing down on her like a crushing burden.

"Mom, Andy," Sydney began, her voice trembling with emotion. "There's something I need to tell you."

Her mom and stepdad turned to face her; concern etched on their faces as they sensed the gravity of her tone.

"What is it, sweetheart?" her mom asked, her voice soft with concern. Sydney took a deep breath, steeling herself for the difficult conversation ahead.

"I... I've been having some health issues," she began haltingly, her words coming out in a rush. "Addison noticed a bald patch on my head last night, and... and it's getting worse." Tears welled up in Sydney's eyes as she struggled to articulate the fear and uncertainty that consumed her. She felt the weight of her mom and Andy's gaze upon her, their silence echoing in the tenseness of the room. For a moment, Sydney feared the worst. Would they react like her dad had, the dismissive laughter and hurtful jokes? Or would they offer the understanding and support she so desperately needed?

As Sydney's words hung heavy in the air, her mom's expression shifted from concern to alarm. Without hesitation, she rushed forward, her eyes scanning Sydney's scalp with a sense of urgency.

"Let me see, sweetheart," her mom said, her voice trembling with worry as she gently parted Sydney's hair to get a closer look. Sydney held her breath, her heart pounding in her chest as she watched her mom's reaction. The weight of her mom's concern was like a balm in her soul, offering a glimmer of hope amidst the darkness of fear. As her mom examined the bald patch on her head, a sense of dread settled over her like a heavy blanket. She could see the worry etched into her mom's features and could feel the tension radiating from her as she took in the extent of her daughter's symptoms.

"It's bad," her mom murmured, her voice barely breaking through as she traced the edges of the bald patch with trembling fingers.

Tears welled up in Sydney's eyes as she nodded, the reality of her situation crashing down on her with crushing force. She had hoped against hope that her mom would have some comforting words of reassurance, but now she realised that the situation was even more dire than she had feared. Grief-stricken, Sydney leaned into her mom's embrace, seeking solace in the comforting warmth of her presence. In that moment, she knew that no matter what lay ahead, she would never have to face it alone. With her mom and stepdad standing by her side, she drew strength and resolve to confront the uncertainties of her future.

"We'll get to the bottom of this, sweetheart," her mom said softly, her voice filled with determination. "We'll find answers and get you the help you need. You're not alone in this."

As Sydney clung to her mom and Andy, she felt a surge of gratitude wash over her. Amid her darkest hour, she found comfort in knowing that no matter what, they would fight these challenges together, as a united front against the storm.

Chapter 7
The Falling Strands

S ydney sat on her bed, a soft light from the evening sun filtering through her window. She glanced at the mirrors across the room but quickly looked away, unable to face her reflection. The once perfect cascade of brown hair that had been her pride and joy now lay in clumps on her pillow, in her brush, and scattered across the floor. Each day seemed to bring a new horror. Every morning, she would wake up to find more hair on her pillow. Every time she ran her fingers through her hair, strands would fall out, slipping through her fingers like sand. It felt like she was losing a part of herself. In a desperate attempt to regain some control, Sydney began collecting the fallen hair. She found a small set of clear bags and gently placed the clumps inside. There was something oddly comforting about it, as if by preserving the hair, she could hold on to a piece of her former self. By the third day, the bags were filling up quickly. Sydney could no longer bring herself to brush her hair, terrified of how much more would come out. Her once lush hair now hung in thin, lifeless strands, and more bald patches began to appear. Each glance in the mirror became more unbearable, the reflection staring back at her was a stranger. The isolation that came with her condition was palpable. Sydney withdrew herself from the world, her house becoming both her sanctuary and her prison. On the sixth day, she stopped leaving the house altogether. The thought of anybody seeing her like this was too much to bear. Addison, Landon, and her other friends and family texted and called, but Sydney couldn't bring herself to respond. She felt isolated, trapped in a prison of her own making. Her mother and Andy tried to be as supportive as possible. They took her to see specialists, hoping for some answers. The doctors ran a battery of tests, but each visit ended with the same uncertainty. "We need to wait for more results," they would say, or "We'll try a different medication." The lack of clear answers only added to Sydney's frustration and despair. By the ninth day, every inch of hair on her body was gone.

Sydney stood in the bathroom, staring at the empty bags lined up on the counter. Her scalp was smooth and bare, and her eyebrows and eyelashes vanished. She looked at her reflection, feeling a pang of sorrow and disbelief. The girl who had once been the epitome of style and confidence was now a shadow of her former self. Tears welled up in her eyes as she touched her bald head, the reality of her situation sinking in fully. She felt a profound sense of loss, not just of her hair but of her identity. Yet, amidst the despair, there was a small glimmer of resilience. She had collected every strand and faced each day's new horror, and somehow, she was still standing. Sydney took a deep breath and turned away from the mirror, determination hardening within her. She didn't know what the future held, but she knew she had to find a way to navigate this new reality. It was time to start piecing together the fragments of her life, one day at a time.

As the days passed, Sydney found solace in small routines. She started wearing scarves and hats to cover her baldness, finding some comfort in the act of dressing up even if it was just for herself. Her mom suggested getting a wig, and after some initial reluctance, Sydney agreed. They went to a wig shop together, and though it was a daunting experience, Sydney found a wig that made her feel a little more like her old self. It wasn't the same, and it irritated her scalp, but it was something. One Friday, Sydney received a call from one specialist they had visited. The doctor had some news. "We've reviewed your case extensively, and while we still don't have all the answers, we believe you may be experiencing Alopecia Universalis. It's an autoimmune condition where the body attacks its own hair follicles." The diagnosis was a mix of relief and new anxiety. While it wasn't life-threatening, the uncertainty of her hair ever growing back was daunting. The doctor discussed potential steroid treatments but made it clear that the condition was unpredictable. With this new information, Sydney decided to take control of her narrative. She researched alopecia, reading stories of others who had faced similar challenges. She joined online support groups, finding comfort in the shared experiences and advice from others who understood her struggle. Addison, true to her promise, remained a constant source of support. She came over whenever possible, bringing with her a sense of normalcy and companionship that Sydney desperately needed. They would watch movies and sit and talk for hours. Addison never treated Sydney differently, and for that, Sydney was immensely grateful.

The day came for Sydney to step out of the confines of her home. Her cousin Sarah's birthday party was the occasion and the thoughts that filled Sydney were nerve-wracking. Sarah was not only her cousin but also one of her closest friends. Only a year apart, they had been inseparable since they were little, sharing countless memories and secrets. Sydney knew that Sarah would be a pillar of support, but the idea of facing everyone without her hair made her stomach churn.

Sydney sat in front of the mirror, running her fingers over her bare scalp. The absence of hair was a true reminder of everything she had been through.

Her mom entered the room, her eyes filled with empathy. "Sydney, you look beautiful," her mom said gently, hugging her tightly.

Sydney looked up, her eyes brimming with uncertainty. "I don't feel beautiful, Mom. I feel exposed."

Her mom knelt beside her, looking into her eyes. "I know it's hard, sweetheart. But remember, you're surrounded by family today. They love you for who you are, not how you look."

Taking a deep breath, Sydney nodded. She chose a soft beanie to wear, one that Addison had given her, and adjusted it carefully. Her mom helped her into a comfortable dress, and together they made their way downstairs. Andy was waiting by the door, the car keys in hand.

He gave Sydney an encouraging smile. "Ready to go, champ?"

"Ready as I'll ever be," Sydney replied, her voice trembling slightly. The drive to Sarah's house felt longer than usual, the anticipation building with each passing mile. When they finally arrived, Sydney hesitated before stepping out of the car. Her mom took her hand, giving it a reassuring squeeze. With a deep breath, Sydney stepped out of the car and walked towards the front door. As soon as they entered, a chorus of warm greetings enveloped her.

Sarah was the first to rush over, her face lighting up with joy.

"Sydney! I'm so glad you came!" Sarah exclaimed, wrapping her in a gentle hug.

Sydney held on tightly, finding comfort in her cousin's embrace. "I wouldn't miss your birthday for anything," she beamed.

Sarah pulled back; her eyes filled with understanding. "You look amazing, Sydney. Come on, let's join the party." Sydney followed Sarah into the living room, where the rest of the family was gathered. The room was decorated with balloons and streamers, and the air was filled with laughter and the smell of delicious food. Despite her initial nerves, Sydney began to relax, feeling the warmth and love radiating from her family. Throughout the party, Sarah stayed by her side, introducing her to guests and making sure she felt comfortable. Sydney's brothers came over to her and kissed her on her head and joined her grandparents and aunts in offering words of encouragement and support. They made her feel welcome, focusing on the joy of the celebration rather than her appearance. The rest of the afternoon passed in a blur of conversation. Sydney found herself relaxing more and more, her initial fears drifting away. She realised that her family saw her for who she was, a strong, resilient person who was fighting her way through a difficult journey. As the party drew to a close, Sydney felt a sense of accomplishment. She had faced her fear and taken significant steps towards reclaiming her life, surrounded by family, and supported by their love.

However, despite her family and Addison's support, the thought of returning to school loomed large in Sydney's mind. She managed to leave the house for Sarah's party but that was just family. Her nerves were frayed, the anticipation of facing her classmates felt like a lead weight in her stomach. The fear of their judgmental looks and whispers was almost too much to bear. She knew that no one could truly understand what she was going through, and that thought made her feel even more isolated.

The night before her return, she barely slept. Her mind was a whirlwind of anxiety and dread. She thought about the comments she might hear, the questions she might be asked. She rehearsed responses in her mind, trying to prepare for every possible scenario. But no amount of preparation could soothe the dreaded fear that she felt.

The morning of her first day back, Sydney stood in front of the mirror, adjusting her headscarf for the hundredth time. Her hands shook slightly as she tried to ensure that it looked as natural as possible. The wig had started to irritate her sensitive scalp, and after some deliberation, she decided that a headscarf was a more comfortable and authentic choice. She chose a soft, patterned scarf that complimented her skin tone and tied it carefully around her head. She took a deep breath and looked at herself, trying to summon some confidence. "You can do this," she whispered to her reflection, hoping to convince herself. Her mom drove her to school, the silence in the car heavy with unspoken worries. As they pulled up to the school, Rachel turned to her daughter and placed a comforting hand on her arm. "You're brave Sydney.

Remember that. And no matter what, you have people who love and support you."

Sydney nodded with a reluctant smile. "Thanks. Mom. I'll be okay."

Chapter 8
Back to School

Sydney stood in front of the school gates, her heart pounding. She took a deep breath, adjusting the scarf once again, and stepped forward. The once familiar halls of Luxton High now felt alien, filled with the weight of her anxiety and the murmurs of students who hadn't seen her in weeks. As she walked down the hallway, she could feel the stares. Whispers followed her like a shadow, blending into a low hum of gossip and speculation. Sydney kept her head high, trying to muster the confidence she once wore so effortlessly. But it was different now; the attention wasn't admiration, but curiosity mixed with pity. Her first stop was her locker. As she fiddled with the lock, she heard snickering from a group of girls nearby. She turned to see them quickly adverse their gazes, pretending to be engrossed in their conversations. Her chest tightened, as she forced herself to focus on her books. The contents of her locker were a comforting constant amid the typhoon of her emotions. She grabbed her textbooks and closed the door, taking another steadying breath.

Walking to her first class, she had never felt more isolated without Addison. Sydney had never felt her best friend's absence more acutely than she did now. Facing this day alone was her worst fear come true. She spotted her boyfriend, Landon, with his friends. He caught her eye and offered her a weak smile, but the boys around him nudged each other and laughed. Sydney's heart sank, but she approached him, hoping for a sense of normalcy.

"Hey, Landon," she said softly.

"Hey, Syd," he replied, but his voice lacked its usual warmth. "How you feeling?"

"Better, I guess," she lied, searching his eyes for reassurance.

One of Landon's friends smirked. "Nice look, Sydney," he said sarcastically with the rest of the group laughing along.

Landon's face flushed, and he glanced at Sydney with an awkward, apologetic look. "Ignore them," he muttered.

Sydney felt a lump form in her throat. "I'll see you later," she said, turning away quickly before he could respond. The pain of his friend's ridicule and his obvious discomfort cut deep. She used to love the attention, but not like this. This was a nightmare.

In her classes, the whispers continued. Sydney could feel eyes on her and hear the muttered conversations that stopped abruptly when she walked by.

In English, she sat alone, the empty seat beside her a stark reminder of her isolation. Her former friends seemed unsure how to approach her, their eyes filled with discomfort and something that looked like sympathy. During lunch, Sydney found a quiet corner in the hall. She picked at her food, her appetite gone. She watched her former friends from a distance, their laughter and animated conversations a painful contrast to her solitude. They hadn't reached out, and she didn't have the strength to approach them. The cafeteria, once a lively place filled with camaraderie, now felt like a battleground. Every laugh seemed directed at her, every glance a judgment. As the day dragged on, Sydney's anxiety grew. She had a biology test next period, and concentrating was almost impossible. The teacher handed out the test papers, and Sydney stared at the questions, her mind blank. She had always been a good student, but today the words seemed to swim on the page. She forced herself to focus, taking deep breaths and tackling one question at a time. It was the only way to push through. After the test, Sydney headed to her next class, maths. As she walked through the door, she saw a group of students huddled together, their heads turning towards her before quickly looking away. She clenched her jaw, determined to get through the class without breaking down. She took her seat and tried to lose herself in the numbers and equations. Maths had always been a refuge, a place where everything made sense and there was always a right answer. Today, it was a lifeline.

The final bell rang, and Sydney gathered her things slowly, hoping to avoid the rush of students leaving. She walked to her locker, the hallways now almost empty, and swapped her books. She was about to close her locker when she felt a tap on her shoulder. She turned to see Mr. Thomas, her Form Tutor, standing with a concerned look on his face.

"Sydney, can we talk for a moment?" he asked gently.

She nodded, following him to his classroom. They sat down, and Mr. Thomas looked at her with genuine concern.

"I've noticed you seem a bit... distracted today,"

he began. "I just wanted to check in and see how you're doing."

Sydney forced a smile. "I'm managing, Mr. Thomas. It's just... been a tough day."

He nodded, understanding. "If you ever need to talk or need some extra time on assignments, don't hesitate to let me know. We're all here to support you in any way."

"Thank you," Sydney said, her voice whist. "I appreciate that."

As she left the classroom, Sydney felt a small measure of relief. It was comforting to know that at least some teachers understood her struggle. But the relief was short-lived. She knew that facing her peers would continue to be a daily battle.

By the end of the day, Sydney was exhausted. She had faced the whispers, the laughter, and the strange looks, but each step had been a battle. She walked home alone, the silence heavy around her. The resilience she had felt while collecting her falling hair was wearing thin, replaced by a deep, aching loneliness. As she reached the front door, Sydney paused, taking a moment to breathe. She knew this was just the beginning. Facing school bald, without her former popularity to shield her, was the hardest thing she had ever done. But she had survived her first day back, tomorrow would be another challenge, but she would face it all one step at a time.

That evening, Sydney lay in bed, staring at her ceiling. Her mind replayed the day's events over and over. The cruel comments, the awkward glances, and the overwhelming sense of isolation. She felt tears welling up in her eyes but blinked them away. She couldn't afford to break down now. Not after she had made it through the day. Her phone buzzed on the nightstand; she picked it up to see a message from Addison.

Addison: Hey, how was your first day back?

Sydney: It was tough. I missed having you there.

Addison: I'm sorry I couldn't be there. I wish I could have been. Do you want to talk about it?

Sydney: Not right now. Just need to process everything. But thank you for checking in.

Addison: Of course. I'm here if you need anything. Just remember, you're stronger than you think.

Sydney put her phone down and closed her eyes. Addison's words were comforting, but the loneliness she felt was heavy. She knew she had to find her own strength to get through this.

Chapter 9
New struggles

The days at Luxton High remained difficult for Sydney. No longer the queen bee, she navigated the hallways as a mere echo of her former self. Her boyfriend and old friends still spoke to her, but she could feel the awkwardness and embarrassment in their voices and actions. They never involved her in their conversations, talking over and around her as if she were invisible. Each day felt like an uphill battle. The only thing that got Sydney through was the thought of seeing Addison after school. The afternoons they hung out together were Sydney's lifeline, a brief escape from the harsh reality of her school life.

One afternoon, as they sat watching the latest episode of their favourite show, Addison noticed red patches on Sydney's arms, "Syd, what's that on your skin?"

Sydney glanced down and sighed. "I don't know. They just appeared out of nowhere. They itch some-times too."

Addison frowned, "You should get that checked out."

Sydney nodded, feeling a sense of unease. Over the next few days, the rashes spread to her face, creating a pattern that some of her so-called friends cruelly commented looked "too perfect," as if she had done it to herself. The gossip hurt, but Sydney tried to ignore it. The intense fatigue was harder to ignore. She found herself exhausted after even the simplest tasks, struggling to stay awake during classes. Her grades started slipping, and she found it hard to concentrate. Every night, she went to bed early, but the fatigue never seemed to leave. One morning, Sydney woke up feeling particularly worn out. She dragged herself out of bed, glancing at the dark circles under her eyes in the bathroom mirror. She was brushing her teeth when she noticed her vision was blurrier than usual. She blinked several times, hoping it would clear, but it didn't. Panic set in when she realised this wasn't a temporary thing. Her parents took her to see a specialist, and the doctor's face was grave as he explained the severity of her symptoms.

"Sydney, I'm afraid you won't be able to drive for the foreseeable future. Your vision is too impaired, and it's not safe."

This news was another blow. Although she had not yet started the process of learning, driving was a symbol of independence, and losing the possibility of that freedom felt like another piece of her identity slipping away. The thought of not being able to drive made her feel even more dependent and trapped.

At school, the whispers grew louder. Her once flawless skin was now marred by rashes, her eyes strained to see the board, and her steps were slower due to the overwhelming fatigue. She could hear the snickers and see the pointing of fingers, but what hurt the most was the change in her friends. They no longer included her in plans, their conversations a series of inside jokes and events Sydney was no longer part of.

"Syd, are you okay?" Landon asked one day, but his eyes were on his friends, who were waiting for him a few steps away.

"I'm fine," Sydney lied, forcing a smile. She knew he felt embarrassed, but he stayed with her out of some sense of obligation rather than genuine care.

The distance between them grew every day, a chasm that neither seemed willing to cross. The isolation at school was suffocating. Sydney would sit alone during lunch, her tray untouched. Her appetite was gone, replaced by a constant knot of anxiety in her stomach.

One Friday, she overheard a group of girls whispering. "Did you see those rashes on her arms? They look so perfect. Do you think she did it to herself for attention?" Sydney's heart sank. She pushed away her tray and left the hall, the words echoing in her mind. It seemed like no matter what she did, the whispers and the stares followed her.

After school, Sydney went to Addison's house for their usual get-together. She arrived before Addi, so she sat on the front steps, staring blankly at her phone. When Addison walked over, Sydney forced a smile, but it quickly crumbled.

Addison immediately noticed. "What's wrong, Syd?"

Sydney's eyes filled with tears. "It's just so hard, Addi. They think I'm doing this to myself for attention, and Landon... he is so distant. I feel like I've lost everything."

Addison reached over and took Sydney's hand in hers. "I'm so sorry Syd. I wish I could be there with you every day. But you have to remember that those people don't define you. You're stronger than this."

Sydney nodded, but the sadness in her eyes remained. "I just don't know how to keep going."

Addison squeezed her hands. "One day at a time. And I'm here for you, always."

The conversation helped, but as Sydney walked home, the weight of her struggles pressed down on her.

At home, she looked at herself in the mirror. The girl staring back was not the confident, popular girl she once knew. The girl who stared back was tired, scared, and uncertain about the future. But somewhere deep inside, there was the flicker of resilience she had faced so much already, telling her she would find a way to navigate through. She turned away from the mirror, took a deep breath, and reached for her phone to text Addison. Despite everything, she knew she wasn't alone.

The next day at school, the challenges continued.

In P.E., Sydney felt more exhausted than usual. Miss. Colby noticed her lagging behind and pulled her aside. "Sydney, you're not looking too good. Are you feeling, okay?"

"I'm just tired," she panted, trying to catch her breath.

"Why don't you sit out for the rest of the class?" Miss. Colby suggested gently.

Sydney nodded, grateful for the reprieve. She sat on the benchers, watching her classmates with a mixture of envy and relief. Her body was betraying her, and there was nothing she could do about it.

During a geography test, Sydney struggled to keep her eyes open. The words blurred together, and she felt a pounding headache coming on. She tried to focus, but it was no use. She turned in her paper early, knowing she hadn't done her best.

Ms. Fields gave her a concerned look as she handed it in. "Everything okay, Sydney?"

"Just really tired," she replied.

"If you need to talk, my door is always open," Ms. Fields said kindly.

Sydney nodded, but she knew talking wouldn't solve her problems. She felt trapped in a body that was failing her, surrounded by people who didn't understand. At lunch, Sydney found her usual corner and sat down with her tray.

Jessica, a quiet girl from her English class, joined her. "Hey, I just wanted to let you know how brave you are. How are you holding up?" she asked, her eyes full of concern.

"I've been better," Sydney admitted, picking at her food.

Jessica nodded. "If you ever need someone to talk to or hang out with, I'm here."

"Thanks, Jessica. That means a lot."

Their conversation was interrupted by a group of girls at the next table, who were laughing loudly. Sydney caught snippets of their conversation and realised they were talking about her. She tried to ignore it, but the words cut deep.

"Looks like she's playing the victim card now."

"Yeah, and those rashes? So fake."

Sydney's hands trembled as she pushed her tray away. Jessica gave the group a sharp look, but they continued to laugh and whisper. Sydney stood up, unable to bear it any longer.

"I'm going to the library," she said, her voice shaky.

Jessica nodded, understanding. Sydney spent the rest of the lunch period hiding in the library, surrounded by books but unable to focus on any of them. The library was her refuge, a place where she could escape the harsh reality of her life for a little while.

The end of the school day brought little relief. As she walked home, the weight of her struggles felt heavier than ever. She tried to remind herself of Addison's words, to take things one day at a time, but it was hard to stay positive.

At home, Sydney's mom noticed the strain on her face.

"How was school today, sweetheart?"

"Rough," Sydney admitted, collapsing to the couch.

Her mom sat down beside her, rubbing her back. "I'm so sorry, honey. I wish there was more I could do."

"Just being here helps," Sydney said, leaning into her mom's comforting touch.

They sat in silence for a while, the only sound was the ticking of the clock. Sydney's mind raced with worries about her health, her friends, and her future. She felt like she was drowning, and she didn't know how to stay afloat.

Later that evening, as she lay in bed, Sydney thought about her conversations with Addison and Jessica. They both offered support, but she still felt so alone. She needed to find a way to cope with everything that was happening, to find her strength again. She picked up her phone and sent a message to Addison.

Sydney: Today was really hard. But I'm trying to stay strong.

Addison: I'm proud of you, Syd. Remember, you're not alone. You've got me, and you've got people who care about you.

Sydney: Thanks Addi. I don't know what I'd do without you.

Addison: You'd still be amazing. You're stronger than you know.

Sydney put her phone down and closed her eyes. Addison's words resonated in her mind, a reminder that she wasn't as alone as she felt. She took a deep breath, trying to summon the resilience she needed.

Chapter 10
The Diagnosis

S ydney's world had been steadily closing in on her. Her eyesight, which had been her primary mode of interaction with the world, was deteriorating rapidly. It began with minor inconveniences, a blur here, a shadow there. At first, she dismissed it, attributing the symptoms to stress or fatigue. However, as weeks turned into months, the blurriness transformed into complete obscurity. Shapes and colours merged into an indistinguishable haze. Even the simplest of tasks, like recognising her parent's faces or reading a text message, became Herculean challenges.

One evening, as Sydney sat at the dinner table with her family, she struggled to follow the conversation. The familiar faces of her mother and stepdad were mere shadows in her vision. The frustration haunted her, a constant reminder of her diminishing independence. She picked at her food, barely listening to the chatter around her. Suddenly, a sharp pain shot through her head, a searing ache that forced her to drop her fork.

"Sydney, are you okay?" her mom asked, worry inscribed in her voice. Sydney pressed her fingers to her temples, trying to massage away the pain.

"It's just a headache," she murmured, though the intensity of the pain was far beyond any headache she'd experienced before.

The headaches started with a dull throb, a constant reminder of her struggles. Over the weeks, they grew more intense, morphing into sharp, stabbing pains that left her clutching her head in agony. Her eyesight, already deteriorating, worsened rapidly. With shapes and colours blurred together, she found it harder and harder to make out even the simplest of objects. Her world was dissolving into a fog of pain and darkness. By now, Sydney was officially registered as blind. The independence she had once cherished was slipping away, replaced by a growing dependence on her parents and the few friends who still cared enough to help. The constant pain and the loss of her vision weighed heavily on her, turning each day into a new struggle.

One night, the pain became unbearable. Sydney awoke with a scream, clutching her head as tears streamed down her face. Her mom and stepdad rushed into her room, their faces pale with fear.

"Sydney, what's wrong?" her mother cried, kneeling beside her bed.

"The pain... it's too much," Sydney gasped, her voice barely recognisable. "I can't take it anymore."

Her stepdad Andy wasted no time, scooping her up and carrying her to the car. The drive to the hospital was a blur. With only Sydney's cries filling the void. Upon arrival, the medical team quickly wheeled her into A&E, her parents following close behind. Doctors and nurses worked quickly, running tests and asking questions Sydney was too dazed to answer. They performed blood tests, CT scans, Lumber Punctures, and rigorous procedures through the groin, which led the doctor to return with the results and a ghostly expression on his face.

"There is a build-up of fluid on her brain," he said. "We need to perform emergency surgery to relieve the pressure immediately."

Sydney's parents nodded, their faces ashen.

"Do whatever you need to do," her stepdad said, gripping his wife's hand.

Sydney was rushed into surgery, the bright lights of the operating room blinding even her failing eyes. The doctors explained the procedure, but the words washed over her in a haze of pain and fear. She felt the pinch of the IV, and moments later, darkness enveloped her as the anaesthesia took effect. The surgery was long and arduous. The surgeons worked with precision, placing an LP shunt in Sydney to continuously drain the excess fluid from her brain. Her parents waited in the sterile, cold waiting room, the minutes stretching to hours. They clung to each other, their minds filled with prayers and desperate hopes.

Finally, the surgeon emerged, pulling down his mask. "The surgery was successful," he said, offering a tired smile. "We've placed a shunt to drain the fluid. She'll need time to recover, but the pressure on her brain should be relieved."

Relief flooded her parents' faces. "Can we see her?" her mom asked, her voice trembling.

"In a little while," the surgeon replied. "We're moving her to recovery now."

Sydney awoke to the soft beeping of monitors and the sterile smell of the hospital room. Her head throbbed with a dull pain, but the intense pressure was gone. She blinked, her vision still a blur but shapes and people noticeable; and she turned her head slightly to see her mom and stepdad sitting beside her bed.

"Mom? Andy?" she croaked; her voice weak.

Her mother leaned forward, tears streaming down her face. "Oh, Sydney, you're going to be okay, sweetheart."

Her stepdad squeezed her hand gently. "The surgery went well."

Over the next few days, Sydney slowly regained her strength. The doctors monitored her closely, adjusting her medications and explaining the details of her condition. Finally, they gave her the diagnosis: Idiopathic Intracranial Hypertension.

"It means there's high pressure in your brain for reasons we can't fully explain," the neurologist said. "The shunt will help manage the fluid, but we will monitor you closely."

Sydney nodded, absorbing the information. It was a lot to take in, but for the first time in weeks, she felt a glimmer of hope. The pain had lessened, and though her vision was still slightly impaired, she knew she had the support of her family and friends. She wasn't facing this battle alone.

In the days that followed, Sydney remained in the hospital, her body weak and her spirit fragile. The doctors reassured her that her symptoms- the stroke, hair loss, headaches, rashes, fatigue, and sight loss- were all her body's response to the fluid build-up in her brain. With the shunt in place, her body can finally begin to heal.

Sydney's parents stayed by her side, their presence a constant source of comfort. Slowly, she started to regain her strength. Physical therapy sessions helped her rebuild muscle, and she began to take tentative steps around the hospital ward. The progress was slow, but each step forward was a victory.

Then, something unexpected happened. One morning, as Sydney brushed her fingers over her head, she noticed something that hadn't been there before: stubble. Her hair was growing back. It started as a fine fuzz, barely noticeable, but day by day, it became thicker and more prominent.

Her mother noticed first. "Sydney, your hair!" she exclaimed, tears of joy in her eyes.

Sydney looked in the mirror, her heart swelling with hope. It felt like a miracle, a sign that her body was truly beginning to heal. She still had a long road ahead, but the blurry sight of her hair returning gave her the strength she needed to keep fighting.

Each day, Sydney pushed herself a little harder. She attended physical therapy sessions with renewed determination, and the doctors marvelled at her progress. Her vision remained impaired, but she learned to navigate the world with the help of her parents and support from her friends.

One evening, as she sat there in her hospital bed, Addison visited, bringing Sydney's favourite snacks.

"Look at you," Addison said, her eyes sparkling. "You're getting stronger every day."

Sydney smiled, reaching up to touch the growing hair on her head. "I guess I am," she said softly. "It's been so hard, but I feel like I'm starting to see the light at the end of the tunnel."

Addison squeezed her hand. "You're the strongest person I know, Syd. You've got this."

Whilst Sydney gazed around the hospital room, she realised that while she had lost so much, she had also gained something invaluable: a deeper understanding of her resilience and the unwavering support of those who loved her. With that, she knew she could face whatever challenges the future brings.

Sydney's road to recovery was marked by small victories and setbacks. Her parents were her constant support, adjusting their lives around her needs. They took turns staying with her in the hospital, coordinating their work schedules to ensure she was never alone. Her older brothers correspondently took turns being by Sydney's side, getting her anything she needed. Nurses and doctors became familiar faces, their encouragement a balm to her wounded spirit.

One afternoon, as Sydney was taking slow steps down the hospital corridor with her physical therapist, she felt a familiar ache in her legs. She paused, leaning against the wall for support. The therapist, a kind woman named Carla, stood beside her.

"You're doing great, Sydney," Carla said gently. "Remember, it's okay to rest when you need to."

Sydney nodded, her breathing heavy. "It's just... I want to get better faster."

"I know you do," Carla replied. "But recovery takes time. You're making incredible progress, even if it doesn't always feel that way."

Sydney took a deep breath and continued her walk. Each step was a reminder of how far she had come and how much further she had to go.

As the weeks turned into months, Sydney's condition stabilised. The shunt effectively managed the fluid build-up, and her pain was significantly reduced. Her hair continued to grow, and her strength slowly returned. Yet, her vision remained impaired, a constant reminder of the challenges she faced.

One sunny afternoon, Sydney's doctors decided she was well enough to leave the hospital. The news was both exhilarating and terrifying. She longed for the comfort of her home but feared the world outside the hospital's protective walls. Her parents prepared for her return, transforming the house to accommodate her needs. They cleared the clutter and made sure her room was safe and accessible. Addison helped, too, bringing over familiar items to make Sydney feel more at ease.

At home, Sydney faced a new set of challenges. The familiar environment now felt foreign, and she had to regain her ability to navigate her own house. Her parents were with her every step of the way, guiding her and helping her regain her independence.

One of the first skills she had to master was the cane. Her physical therapist, Carla, recommended a specialist who worked with visually impaired individuals. Her name was Valery, and she came to their house twice a week to teach Sydney how to use one.

"Hold it like this," Valery instructed, placing the cane in Sydney's hand. "It should be an extension in your arm. Sweep it from side to side in front of you using the muscles in your wrist."

Sydney tried, but the movements felt awkward and uncertain. Valery was patient, guiding her hands and offering encouragement.

"It takes time, Sydney. You'll get the hang of it."

Her parents watched from the sidelines, their expressions a mix of worry and pride.

Each session was a step toward independence, but it was also a stark reminder of how much had changed. As the weeks passed, Sydney became more comfortable with the cane, but it also gave her a lot of anxiety. However, Valery said that once she learned specific routes, the cane could be held as a symbol cane. Sydney's parents or Addison always accompanied her on routes, offering guidance and reassurance.

Another essential skill Sydney had to learn was touch typing. She had always been a fast typist, but now she had to rely solely on her sense of touch. She was given a specialised keyboard with raised dots on the keys from the Society for the Blind, which she had been practising on daily. At first, it was frustrating. Her fingers fumbled over the keys, and mistakes were frequent. But she persevered, her determination fuelled by the desire to regain some semblance of normalcy.

One day, as she sat at her desk, she managed to

type a full paragraph without a single error. Her mom, who had been watching, clapped her hands in delight.

"You did it, Sydney! I'm so proud of you!"

Sydney smiled, a sense of accomplishment washing over her. Each small victory was a reminder that she could adapt and overcome the challenges she faced.

Reading Braille was another skill Sydney needed to master. The Society for the Blind set up lessons with one of their specialists.

The instructor, Ms. Jenson, was a patient and experienced teacher. "Braille is a tactical writing system," Ms. Jenson explained during the first class. "Each cell is made up of six dots, and the arrangement of those dots represents different letters and symbols." Sydney's fingers brushed over the raised dots on the page, trying to decipher the patterns. It was challenging, but she was determined to learn. Ms. Jenson provided individual attention, helping Sydney develop her tactical reading skills.

As the weeks went by, Sydney's proficiency in Braille improved. She practised daily, her parents, brothers and Addison providing encouragement. One evening, she was able to read a short story written in Braille. It was a significant milestone, filling her with a sense of pride and achievement.

Throughout this journey, Sydney's dependence on her parents, brothers, and best friend was a constant reality. They accompanied her everywhere, ensuring her safety and providing support. It was a difficult adjustment for all of them, but their bond grew stronger through the shared challenges. Her mom, Rachel, was always intensive and helped with daily tasks and encouraged Sydney to keep pushing forward. Andy, her stepdad, was a steady presence, his quiet strength a comfort in the face of uncertainty. Her brothers, Brandon and Noah, were her constant beck and call, getting her anything she needed. And Addison's constant visits brought joy and a sense of normalcy, her laughter a welcome reprieve from the struggles.

One afternoon, as they sat together after a physical therapy session, Sydney turned to her parents.

"Thank you," she said, her voice filled with emotion. "I couldn't have done this without you."

Her mom smiled, tears in her eyes. "We love you, Sydney. We'll always be here for you."

Andy nodded. "You're a fighter, Syd. You've come so far, and we are so proud of you."

That evening, Sydney felt around her room. It was filled with reminders of her journey, photos of her friends and family, and cards and letters of encouragement. She had come so far, and while there were still challenges ahead, she knew she could face them with the support of her loved ones and the strength she had discovered within herself.

Chapter 11
A New Beginning

Sydney's road to recovery was slow but steady. Each day presented new challenges and triumphs as she navigated her way through a world that had drastically changed. One step in her journey was joining an in-person support group where she met other teens facing similar challenges. They shared stories of their struggles and triumphs, creating a bond that gave Sydney a sense of belonging she hadn't felt in a long time.

The first friend Sydney met was Naomi. They were the same age, both grappling with significant health challenges that had turned their worlds upside down. Naomi had also lost her hair due to a complex brain issue that mirrored Sydney's own struggles. The two girls bonded instantly, finding solace in their shared experiences. Naomi was a vibrant soul, her spirit unbroken despite the physical and emotional toll of her condition. She had a contagious energy that lifted Sydney's spirits during their group sessions. They spent hours discussing their school lives, the challenges of being young girls dealing with health issues, and how their families had rallied around them. Naomi's family, like Sydney's, had been incredibly supportive, creating a network of love and care that helped her through the darkest times.

"We're like warriors," Naomi would often say, her eyes shining with determination. "We've been through so much, but we're still here, still fighting."

Sydney nodded, feeling a surge of strength from Naomi's words. "You're right. And we have each other now, too."

The support group was a melting pot of stories, each member bringing their unique perspective and strength to the table. Sydney met other teens who, like her, had lost their sight or were dealing with various health issues. Each meeting was a blend of tears, laughter, and shared wisdom. There was Uzma, a girl with an infectious sense of humour despite her own struggles with sight loss. Uzma had a knack for finding humour in everyday challenges. She shared tips and tricks on navigating the world without sight, from using a cane to relying just on the auditory cues in the environment.

"Listen, Sydney," Uzma said during one session, "the world isn't just what you see, it's what you hear, what you feel, even what you smell. Learn to use all your senses, and you'll find your way."

Then there was Megan, a girl who had been blind since birth. Megan was a wellspring of knowledge about living a full life despite her blindness. She introduced Sydney to various adaptive technologies and techniques that made everyday tasks more manageable.

"Technology is your friend," Megan advised, demonstrating a screen reader on her phone. "It can open up so many possibilities for you."

Through these interactions, Sydney learned valuable skills that helped her regain a sense of independence.

One of the most significant benefits of the support group was the shared understanding of the emotional toll their conditions took. They discussed the frustrations of dealing with insensitive remarks from peers, the exhaustion from medical treatments, and the grief of losing certain abilities. As weeks turned into months, the bond between Sydney and her new friends grew stronger. They supported each other through medical appointments, celebrated milestones, and shared countless conversations that deepened their connection. The friendships Sydney forged in the support group became a source of strength as she faced the challenges of her final school year and the prospect of moving forward with her life. They had shown her that she wasn't defined by her blindness or her medical condition but by her resilience, her ability to adapt, and the love and support she gave and received.

Returning to school was a daunting prospect. Sydney had missed a significant amount of time, and the thought of facing her peers again filled her with anxiety. However, she also felt a newfound determination. She was not the same person she had been before her diagnosis and surgery. She had faced immense challenges and had come out stronger on the other side. It was time to show the world who she truly was. Her first day back was a mixture of nerves and excitement. Sydney's parents drove her to school, offering words of encouragement as they pulled up to the familiar building.

"You've got this, sweetheart," her mom said, squeezing her hand. "Remember, we are so proud of the woman you have become."

Sydney nodded, taking a deep breath. "Thanks,

mom. Thanks, Andy." She stepped out of the car, clutching her cane for support. The cane had become a symbol of her independence, guiding her through the world she was still learning to navigate. The hallways were filled with the sounds of usual morning activity, but as Sydney made her way to class, she could feel eyes on her. Whispers followed her down the corridor, but she held her head high, determined not to let them affect her. She worked hard to get to this point, not to be deterred by idle gossip.

The first few days were challenging. Sydney had to adjust to the new ways of learning and navigating the social dynamics of her peers. Some students were supportive and curious, asking respectful questions about her condition and how they could help. Others were less considerate, either avoiding her altogether or making insensitive comments. Sydney chose to focus on the positive interactions, leaning on both friends who stood by her and the new connections she was making.

Although Sydney faced school with a new profound confidence, that didn't mean it was easy. She encountered numerous obstacles, one of the biggest being her GCSE exams. Being blind meant she needed extra time in exams with a reader and scribe, which often meant spending the whole day focussing on one test. It was mentally and physically exhausting, but Sydney refused to let it hold her back. She persevered, determined to prove that her blindness wouldn't define her. Her teachers were supportive, going out of their way to make sure she had everything she needed to succeed. They provided materials in Braille and set up voice-to-text software to help her keep up with her studies. One teacher who stood out as a beacon of support was her English teacher, Mrs. Harrod. From the moment Sydney returned to school, Mrs. Harrod had been there for her, offering guidance, encouragement, and immense support. She recognised Sydney's potential from the beginning. Despite the challenges of being blind, Sydney's determination to excel in her studies never wavered. Mrs. Harrod went above and beyond to ensure that Sydney had everything she needed to succeed and offered extra support and help whenever she needed it. However, her English teacher's support extended far beyond the classroom. She became a trusted confidant and mentor to Sydney, always there to lend a listening ear or offer words of wisdom. Their bond grew stronger with each passing day. Sydney knew that no matter what obstacles she faced, Mrs. Harrod would be there to help her overcome them. Sydney studied hard, pouring over textbooks and lesson notes, determined to absorb as much information as possible. It was a challenging process, but her family was there throughout it all, and although they lacked knowledge of the subjects, they helped in any way they could. When the exam results came in, Sydney was overjoyed to find that she had passed with flying colours. The news spread quickly through the school, earning her admiration from teachers and classmates alike.

But there was still some unfinished business Sydney needed to overcome. She decided it was time to confront her so-called friends and set the record straight. She gathered them together after school one day, her heart pounding but her resolve firm.

"Look," she began, her voice steady. "I know things have been weird between us, and I get it— my life changed a lot, and so did I. But that doesn't mean I did anything wrong. I'm still the same person, and I deserve friends who respect and support me." Her friends shifted uncomfortably, but Sydney didn't back down. "I won't tolerate being treated like an outsider anymore. If you can't accept me for who I am now, then maybe we're better off going our separate ways."

The confrontation was a turning point. Some of her friends apologised and promised to do better, but Sydney knew it was time to let go of those who couldn't be supportive. Among them was Landon, her boyfriend, whose distant and unsupportive behaviour had only added to her struggles.

"Landon," Sydney said, taking a deep breath, "this isn't working anymore. I need someone who stands by me, not someone embarrassed to be with me."

Landon looked stunned but didn't argue. "I understand," he said quietly. "I'm sorry, Sydney."

With that chapter of her life closed, Sydney felt a weight lift off her shoulders. She focussed on the positive relationships in her life, including her friendship with Addison, who had been incredibly supportive throughout.

As prom dawned closer, and with Addison being her plus one, it was time for them both to look for a dress. The process of shopping was an adventure in itself, with Sydney relying on her mom and Addison to help go through the different styles and colours. They spent hours in the dressing room, laughing and bonding over their shared excitement for their big night.

Prom night arrived, and Sydney felt a mix of excitement and nervousness. As she got ready, her family helped her with every detail. Her mom did her hair, and Addison did her makeup as well as her own, whilst Andy and her brothers stood in the background, making sure the dress was perfect and every detail was right. Her dress was a vision of elegance and sophistication. It was a beautiful off-the-shoulder cream two-piece ensemble that perfectly accentuated her figure. The top featured delicate silk detailing, adding a touch of romanticism, while the bottom flowed gracefully to the floor, creating an ethereal effect as she moved. The waist was clinched in with a detailed belt, highlighting Sydney's slender frame and adding a touch of glamour to the overall look. To complement her stunning dress, Sydney chose glittery gold heels that added a hint of sparkle to her ensemble. The heels matched perfectly with the gold accents in her dress, adding a subtle yet stylish touch to her outfit. With every step she took, the heels glimmered in the light, adding an enchanting aura that surrounded her. As a final touch, Sydney adorned her wrist with the most beautiful corsage. The delicate flowers added a pop of colour to her outfit, complementing the cream tones of her dress perfectly. With each moment, the corsage swayed gently, adding a whimsical touch to Sydney's overall look. Sydney's hair, now chin length, was styled in a glamorous half-updo. Loose curls cascaded down her, framing her face and adding a soft, romantic touch to her appearance. To add a touch of flair to her hairstyle, Sydney added gold flower clips, adding a striking detail that tied the entire look together.

Addison twirled in her dress, a beautiful crimson red that complemented her eyes beautifully. "You look amazing, Syd," she said, her voice filled with genuine admiration.

As Sydney looked at the blurred version of herself in the mirror, she couldn't help but smile.

Her mother took a step back, tears glistening in her eyes. "You look beautiful, sweetheart. Tonight is your night."

Sydney felt confident, beautiful, and ready to take on the world. With her stunning dress, sparkling heels, and glamorous hairstyle, she knew that she was ready to make a grand entrance at prom and dance the night away with her friends.

When she was about to leave for prom, Sydney felt a flutter of nerves as she stepped out of the house, but as soon as she saw the Bentley her dad had hired waiting for her, excitement took over. Her dad had recently gotten in touch to apologise for the way he and her stepfamily reacted to her illness, and although still not close, she understood that he loved her and tried to support her in a way that he could. With her family and Addison by her side, she climbed into the car, feeling like a princess on her way to the ball. As they arrived at the venue, Sydney felt a surge of adrenaline. She could hear the music and laughter from inside and couldn't wait to join the festivities. As she entered the room, whispers and glances followed her, but this time, they were different. There was admiration and respect in the eyes of her peers. Sydney's heart raced as she felt the atmosphere change. She could sense the admiration in the room. Students who had once looked at her with pity or curiosity now saw her as a symbol of strength and resilience. Teachers who had supported her journey beamed with pride. She moved through the crowd with Addison by her side, feeling the warmth of smiles and the buzz of conversations around her. Some students came up to her, complimenting her dress and expressing how glad they were to see her. It was overwhelming in the best possible way. When Sydney and Addison hit the dancefloor, it was as if all her worries melted away. She moved to the rhythm of the music, feeling a sense of freedom and joy that had eluded her for so long. Friends, old and new, joined them, creating a circle of laughter and fun. Sydney danced and laughed, feeling truly happy for the first time in a long while. The weight of her struggles seemed to lift as she twirled and swayed, surrounded by people who admired and respected her strength and perseverance.

As she stood with her friends and family, she realised how far she had come. She was no longer the girl who needed to fit in to feel accepted. She had found strength within herself and learned the value of true friendship and support. She knew now that the girl she had started as, who thrived off attention and being the most popular girl in the school, didn't carry the depth and knowledge she had gained through her experiences.

As the night drew to a close with a final dance, Sydney stood in the middle of the dancefloor, feeling a sense of fulfilment. She had faced immense challenges and emerged stronger. With her GCSEs behind her and her future ahead, she knew she could handle whatever life threw her way. Sydney had come a long way from the girl she used to be, and she was ready to embrace the next chapter of her life with confidence and hope. The support group, her family, Addison, and even the respect of her peers had shown her that she was capable of greatness. Prom night was a testament to her journey, and as she left the venue, hand in hand with Addison, she felt like the true queen bee she was meant to be.

About the Author

Shelby Benson draws from her own experiences in crafting the poignant narrative of "Echoes of Reflection." Having weathered similar storms during her own teenage years, She brings a deeply personal touch to the story of Sydney, the protagonist grappling with adversity amidst the complexities of high school life. Through her writing, Shelby captures the essence of resilience, drawing upon her own journey to infuse authenticity and depth into Sydney's tale. " Echoes of Reflection" stands as a testament to Shelby Benson's ability to transform personal challenges into compelling narratives that resonate with readers on a profound level. Beyond her literary pursuits, Shelby is a university graduate, a fiancée, and is currently pursuing a career in education, driven by her desire to serve as a mentor and inspiration to the next generation, just as others once did for her.